BLUFFTON

MY SUMMERS WITH BUSTER

MATT PHELAN

CANDLEWICK PRESS

First edition 2013

Library of Congress Catalog Card Number 2012947260
ISBN 978-0-7636-5079-7

13 14 15 16 17 18 TLF 10 9 8 7 6 5 4 3 2 1

Printed in Dongguan, Guangdong, China

This book was typeset in Humana Sans.
The illustrations were done in watercolor.

Candlewick Press
99 Dover Street
Somerville, Massachusetts 02144

visit us at www.candlewick.com

For Nora and Jasper

HARRISON'S
631
TIC
TIC
JUNE
1908
Life in Muskegon, Michigan,
was quiet. Ordinary.

Sure, Pop.
See you back home for supper, Henry.
But that all changed in the summer of 1908.

The summer *they* arrived.

The vaudevillians. Show people. Here to spend the summer by our lake.

BUSTER!

You there, young Muskegonite!
S-sir?
Is that the trolley line to Bluffton?
Yes, sir. Last stop.
Thanks, kid.

OK, folks, make room. Just . . . OK, now . . . please.
Better wait for the next one, Henry. No room for you here.
OK, Mr. Crosby.
And for those few months of summer, nothing would be ordinary.

Hey, Sally. Bet you can't guess what I just saw —
An elephant.
That's right.
Mother said the vaudeville performers were arriving today. Said they had an elephant and a zebra.

That so?
They're renting cottages in Bluffton this summer. On vacation.
All summer?

That's what Mother says.
Well . . . bye, Sally.
Bye, Henry.

Henry, fetch
your brother.

Bluffton was the name of the small neighborhood
on the western bank of Muskegon Lake.

Bluffton was right by the last trolley stop at the foot of Pigeon Hill (the bluff). Everybody took that trolley because it was also the stop for Lake Michigan Park, a short stroll away.
Bluffton
Muskegon Lake
Lake Michigan Park
Streetcar to Downtown Muskegon
Lake Michigan
My neighborhood
Of course, I'd been to Lake Michigan Park many times.
But I'd never been to Bluffton.

COBWEBS &
RAFTERS
OFFICIAL CLUBHOUSE
OF THE
ACTORS' COLONY

CRASH!
WHY I OUGHTA...!

...hee-hee
SHH!
[snicker]
hee...

Sand breaks the fall.
It's like landing on a pillow.

I'm Buster. That's Jingles and Louise.
Henry.
You live around here?
In Muskegon.
Isn't it swell?
I . . .
I guess.
You play ball?
Sure.
Tomorrow. Ten sharp. By Pascoe's. Bring some kids.

Hey, kid! C'mere.
Do me a favor. Go in there and grab me a pop from the ice chest, will ya?
Yes, sir.
I'd get it myself, but seeing as how you were already standing . . .

Much obliged.
COBWEBS & RAFTERS
OFFICIAL CLUBHOUSE OF THE ACTORS' COLONY
You know, technically I shouldn't let you up here. This is the official Actors' Colony clubhouse.
You like vaudeville, son?
I've never been to a show.
Jumping Jehosophat.

Have a seat, young local yokel, and allow me, Ed Gray, Noted Monologuist, to elucidate on the subject at hand.

Here at the Actors' Colony, we have only the top talent, mind you. No medicine-show hucksters, road-show hacks, or tent-show miscreants here.

No, my good fellow, here we are the cream of the crop, the mainstays of the glorious two-a-day theaters, the pride of the Keith Circuit!

Vaudeville is variety.

A veritable calvacade of comedians, jugglers, dancers, magicians, acrobats, musicians, and dramatic actors . . . all for short, precise acts of the highest entertainment value!

A day in the theater promises twelve to fifteen acts to amuse, inspire, electrify, edify, and enlighten (for one small price).

You'll see things your eyes won't believe. SUCH AS —
Will Ferry, the Frog Man! The greatest contortionist who ever bent a rubber limb!
Sandow, the strongest man on earth!
Peg Leg Bates, the one-legged tap dancer!
Nora Bayes, the world's finest singing comedienne!
Bert Williams, the greatest Negro funny man!

And then the star of the bill takes the stage at the next-to-closing act –
Why isn't the star last?
Why isn't the . . . ? Wha–? The last act is filler, boy. Something to play while the dear audience gathers their things and legs it. No, no. You've reached the top when you're Next-to-Closing.
Lemme give you an example.
Have you met Buster?
Is his father a star?
His father? Well, sure, Joe Keaton IS a star. His act is the Three Keatons.
But he'd be the first to tell you: everyone knows to keep your eye on the kid.

Buster crawled onstage during his dad's act when he was but a babe. And he got a laugh. By age four, he was part of the act.
Whew! And WHAT an act!
The Three Keatons are the wildest knockabout act in the business.
They call Buster "the human mop."

The kid's indestructible. He can take a fall better than anyone alive.
HA
HA
HA!
HA-HA
And the kicker?
HA!
Buster never cracks a smile. Ever. No matter what. That's what really makes it funny.
HA
HA
HA!
HA-HA
HA!

And that is but a small taste of the glories of vaudeville.
Like I said, some of the biggest stars of all are here this summer enjoying the tranquility of Muskegon Lake, as the vaudeville houses are closed due to sweltering heat.
Last time the Three Keatons played Muskegon, Joe discovered Bluffton.
"Ed," he said to me, "it's a slice of heaven!"
Ain't it the truth?

DOWNTOWN
MUSKEGON

3¢
Sounds like some two-penny nails would do it.
Yep.
3¢

3¢
3¢
3¢
3¢

Thanks, Al.
See you, now.
Well, Henry, what have you been up to this fine summer day?
I . . . uh . . . I went up to Bluffton.
Meet the show people?
It's an Actors' Colony. It even has a clubhouse!
That so?

Sure! I met one of the stars of the Three Keatons! He's about my age, too.
Three Keatons? Hmmm. I've seen them.
You have?! Where?

At the theater at Lake Michigan Park. Must have been three years ago.
Why didn't you take me?
Take you? You were too young.
They were . . . what do you call it? A knockabout act. Pretty rough. They threw that kid around like he was a sack of flour.

It was funny, though. Right?
Well, sure. But I still couldn't help but worry a little about that boy. It was a school night, too.
Now, how about you give me a hand and let's get home to supper?

The next day, I went back to Bluffton with some kids from my neighborhood.
Lex
Mike
Emmet
Sam
Billy
Tom
Henry
Buster
Joe
Carl

Everyone got along.
Baseball does that.
Buster had his own style of playing.

He couldn't get enough of baseball. He'd play all day and all night if he could.
I stayed longer than my pals.

And eventually . . .
I was the only kid in my neighborhood who wanted to hike up to Bluffton every day.
I was becoming an honorary Actors' Colony kid. Eating fried perch at Pascoe's . . .
swimming in the lake . . .
fishing . . .
and doing a lot of nothing. Typical summer stuff.

Nah. I'm not in my folks' act. I just travel with 'em. Someday I'll be up there. Might be a monologuist or a comic. But I'll leave the falls to this knucklehead.

Maybe you could show me that flip thing, Buster.
You have to learn how to fall. Otherwise you get hurt. Bad. A catastrophe.
You don't have to be onstage for catastrophe to hit. Sometimes it just follows you around.
See this?

When I was three, I wandered out back of the boardinghouse where we were staying to watch a girl wring clothes.
That wringer fascinated me.
So I stuck my finger in it.

Crushed it. Doc comes over and cuts off the finger to the first joint.
He bandages the finger, and I cry myself to sleep.
I wakc up a few hours later and go back out exploring.
There's a peach tree. And I wanted a peach.
So I toss a brick up at it.

BAM! Doc comes back. Three stitches in my scalp.
Back to bed with me. Well, I get out of bed again, this time because of a noise.
Kansas twister!

It sucks me out the window . . .
carries me down the block . . .
and sets me down easy as can be.

A man scoops me up and takes me to a storm cellar.
When it was over, the man brought me back to Mom and Dad, who had been understandably concerned.
After that day, my folks figured I could survive anything we did onstage.

Late afternoons often found the gang at Cobwebs & Rafters . . .

Is this about the fish
I caught today?
Layabout!
Uh-oh. Speaking
of fish . . .

That's Mr. Spanner,
our principal.

Whirrrrr!

Holy smokes! It's a big one! Don't let go!
Well, I—
Let out your line!
Jerk him to the left! The left!
You'll never forgive yourself if you lose him!

YANK
Oof!
?

HA
HA
Ho
HA
Hee
HA
HA
Ha
HA
HA
HA
HA
HA
HA

Just a gag, friend.
No harm intended.
A gag?
You see, the line drops down here through a pulley weighted at the bottom by a rock.
It runs under the dock and up into the clubhouse.

My boy Buster figured it all out.
Hmmph.
Men, I think this calls for some refreshment at Pascoe's!

PLOP!
sigh

Can't believe summer's almost over.
And then school starts again.
Say, Buster. How do you go to school when you're on the road?
I don't.

Ever?
I went once.
One day.
That's it.
First thing, the teacher took roll call.
"Smith?" "Here!"
"Johnson?" "Here!"
"Keaton?"
"I couldn't come today."
Everybody laughed, even the teacher.

So, I thought school was great. Just an extra show a day.
I had a joke for every class. The kids roared, but the teachers started to frown.
In grammar, the teacher asked for a sentence with the word *delight* in it.
I answer, "The vind blew in de vindow and blew out de light."

Next thing I know, I'm being led to the principal's office.
Sent me home with a note: "Do not send this boy to school again."
That was that.
But I learn loads of stuff from the other performers, so . . .

That summer held one more event of note.
Joe Keaton's birthday . . .
celebrated vaudeville style.

That was the first summer.

sigh

Lex was traveling with his parents, so he got to watch all of the shows. He sent me detailed descriptions.

Even when he was little, Buster had been dressed up to fool the authorities. Joe spread the rumor that he was a midget.

With some help from their many friends . . .
Say, how old is he?
they mostly got away with it.
I dunno. You'll have to ask his wife.

But lately, the Gerry Society had doubled their efforts.
And it fell to Joe Keaton to prove that Buster wasn't getting hurt in the act.

Lex told me in a letter that the Gerry Society had been successful.

Back in 1907, the Three Keatons had been banned from performing on the biggest New York stages for two years.

Buster hadn't mentioned that last summer.
Of course, Buster hadn't really talked about his life onstage at all.
Gee.

SUMMER, 1909

Ed Gray keeps ignoring his alarm clock, so he asked Buster to help him out. It's about to start.
What's about to start?
The Awakener.

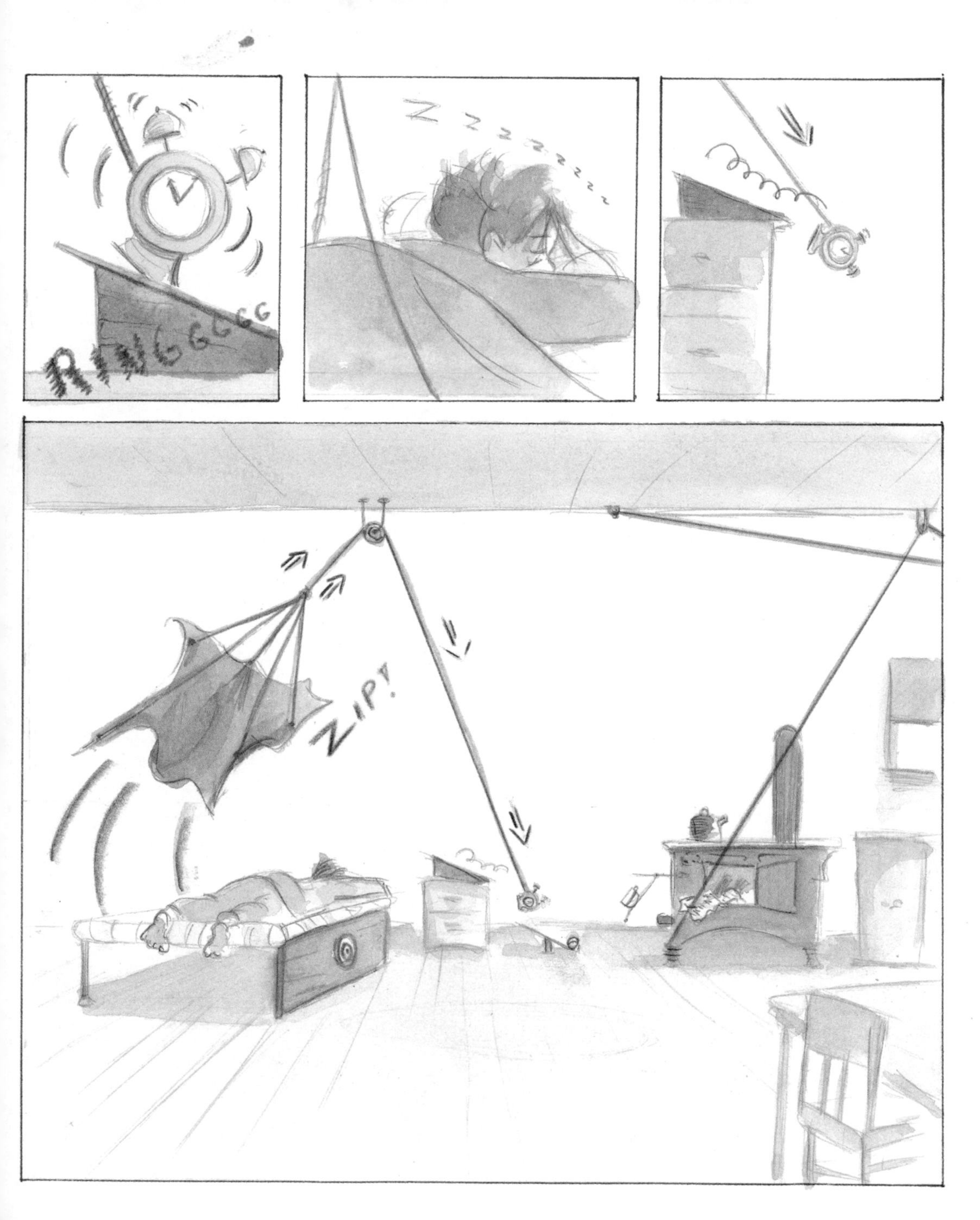
Z z z z z z z z z
ZIP!

Here we go. . . .
SCRITCH!

Ed has thirty seconds to shut it off or else.
He never shuts it off in time.
SNAP

BAM!
!

Morning,
boys.
Tweeeee!

Bluffton picked up right where we left off the year before.

The only difference was that there were even more vaudevillians this summer. They packed into the Bluffton Boardinghouse on Wilcox Street . . .

and added to the stories and mayhem at Cobwebs & Rafters.

Buster's mom had plenty of friends for her constant pinochle game.

The days were again filled with baseball . . .
fishing for perch . . .
and loitering.
Buster hardly ever stopped. It was like he was trying to smush a whole summer into every single day.

Hi,
Henry.

Hi, Sally. Hi, Mary.
What are you doing?

Pulling Mary in the wagon.
That's it?
Yes.

I've been up at Bluffton. Playing with Buster. He's a star –
I know who he is. I saw his act once.
You – what? When?

A few years ago at Lake Michigan Park. His father throws him around the stage, and they hit each other.
It looked like it would hurt, but he seemed all right at the end.
He didn't smile. It was kind of sad.

Sad? He doesn't smile on purpose. It's funnier that way!
Oh?
Of course! That's showmanship. They're professionals. They're . . . they're STARS!

I suppose. He still seemed a little sad to me.
Bye, Henry.
Hmmph!

HENRY!
Big delivery today. I'll need you for a few hours.
Yes, sir.

OK, son.

The Keatons had started calling their cabin Jingles' Jungle because of Buster's brother's toys being everywhere. The cabin was sparse, no indoor plumbing or anything, but Buster loved it.

The boardinghouses aren't all bad.
Zeiser's in Philadelphia is nice.
I like Mother Howard's
in Baltimore.
She sure can cook. My
favorite is the Ehric House.
Oh, Ehric's
is great.
Where is the
Ehric House?

It's in New York City.
Our first hotel fire was in Ehric's.
First?
Yeah. Pop was at the saloon, but when Mom asked, I said I didn't know where he was. Me and Mom got out with Jingles and Louise in time.
Then there was the Canobie Lake Hotel near Salem, New Hampshire.

And then there was the Lake Hotel outside of Toledo.
And Sioux City, Iowa. That one caught Mom in the bath. Boy, was she mad.
But the fires are nothing compared to all the train wrecks.
Train wrecks?

Say, Buster. Who came up with the rope-and-ball gag?
Pop mostly. I added a bit of timing, I guess.
What's the rope-and-ball gag?
Our big finish to the act. Pop's onstage shaving at a mirror.
His back's to me. I climb up on the table . . .

with a weighted ball on
the end of a long rope.
I keep swinging the ball,
letting out more rope.
It gets closer . . . and
closer. Building. Building.
The audience laughing more
and more with each swing.

POW!
Pop hits the mirror. Then he goes after me and finally tosses me into the orchestra pit.
It's the best!
There's nothing like it. The laughs. The applause. I can't get enough of it.

Show me something. Teach me a flip or a fall.
Oh, I don't know, Henry. . . .
It takes a lot of practice.
I can practice!
You can get hurt pretty bad if—
Come on!
OK. Come here.

You could break your neck with a flip, so we'll start with a fall.
The thing is to tense the right muscles while keeping the rest of the body relaxed.
Ummm . . .
If you're tense all over, you'll break something. If you're too relaxed, you won't land correctly and . . . well, you'll break something that way, too.

This is a simple gag. Lean back as far as you can without falling.
Now walk backwards like that.
Here's the gag. I sweep under you as you move back . . .
and then I'm going to take your legs out. Tense your stomach. Bring your legs up high, and relax into the fall. Tense and relax. Got it?
I—

WHACK!
WHUMP
How'd it go?
OOFF!
Winded.
Uh . . . huh . . .
Give it a second.

OK, Henry. Now let's do something important.
BASEBALL!
But—

No summer would be complete without days spent at Lake Michigan Park, a short walk from the Bluffton trolley stop.

Everyone in Muskegon came to the park.

Henry!
Henry Harrison!

Hi, Sally!

Sally, this is Buster and Lex.
Sally is my neighbor.

How do you do?
Just fine. Fine and dandy.
Well . . . I guess we better head in, huh?

There was plenty to do at the park.
C'MON, BIG JOE!

HA HA HA
HA
HA HA
HA
HA-HA
HA
HA
HA
HA
HA
HA
HA

SPIN
SPIN
SPIN
HA-HA-HA
HA-HA-HA
HA!
HA
HA
HA-HA
HA
Sometimes the vaudevillians just couldn't help themselves.

Where's Buster?
Buster!

There seemed to be more vaudevillians every day.
Some would just stay a few days at the boardinghouse.
And they would all end up at Pascoe's.
Dixon and Fields
Samaroff and Sonia

Bill "Bojangles"
Robinson

Holy cow . . .
Is that—?
Sure is.
Harry Houdini, the Handcuff King.

Pop's known Houdini since their medicine-show days. I've watched his act a million times, and I can't figure out how he escapes.
Buster!
I gave him that name, you know.

He was just baby Joseph. We were staying at a rickety hotel on the road. One day there was a **CRASH** on the staircase.
I rush over with Joe, and there's the baby at the bottom of the stairs. Fell down a full flight!
We look and he's all right. "My, what a Buster!" I say.
And he's been Buster ever since.

And he's been hounded ever since. By the Gerry Society.
Now, Joe . . .
Protection of children. HA! Do you know how many poor kids are living on the streets of New York? Hungry every night? Orphans, kids kicked around by fathers who mean to hurt them. Do they save them? No! They bother us.

We are actors! Buster's never been hurt in his life.
Well, not bad, anyway.
I think you've had enough, old friend.
Yes. I believe I have, Mr. Handcuff King.

What a card!

Houdini! HARRY Houdini!
You don't say.
Harry Houdini!
I heard you, son.

Most days in Bluffton drifted by without a care.
But occasionally there were days with a purpose.
I get hikers, mostly. People wandering by. Just because you can see my outhouse from the trail doesn't mean there's an open invitation to use it. A man likes his privacy.
Can you help me out, Buster?

Pssst!

Curtain time.
TUG!
!

Problem solved,
Buster.

That was something Buster, even for you.
Yeah! How did you figure out how to rig that?
Oh, I don't know . . .
I think if anybody asked me, I'd tell them I wanted to be a civil engineer some day.

Of course . . . no one ever asks me.

As the days went by, I'd try desperately to get Buster to show me more stunts and gags.
But he always changed the subject.
Most of the vaudevillians spent time practicing their acts.

But Buster wasted a lot of time doing not much of anything.
Sometimes I thought he didn't appreciate how good he had it.
Henry, I'm going to need you at the store tomorrow. All day.
Sure, Pop.

I'll close up, Henry. Thanks for your help today.
OK, Pop. See you later.

Hello.
Oh! Hi, Henry.
Buster's here.
I can see that.
Lemonade!
I hope you like
oatmeal cookies,
Buster dear.
Henry.

Hello, Mrs. Conners.
That was the last of the lemonade.
Oh, that's OK. Thank you.
Were you working at your store today?

My father's store.
I had invited Buster to visit one day. Just to see where we lived.
These are nice houses – homes, I mean.
Maybe you'd like to visit Jingles' Jungle. It's not . . . well . . . it has a swell view of the lake and –
It's just I'm surprised to see you two getting along. I wouldn't have thought it.

What do you mean, Henry?
Well, Sally, you're at the head of our class, love reading, might even be a teacher someday . . .
and Buster . . . I mean, he's only been to school one day in his whole life.
Henry Harrison.

Thank you for the cookies, Sally. I should be going.

Buster, I hope you visit again soon.

Well, I . . .

I didn't know exactly
why I said what I said.
I was mad.
Mad at Buster.
Mad at myself.
Mad about everything he had . . .
Everything I wanted.

I didn't go back to Bluffton the next day.
Or the next.
Two weeks went by . . .

before I returned.
Lex told me that Buster had been spending a lot of time playing with his little brother lately.
And playing ball with the grown-ups.
Something else had happened while I was away. . . .

Joe Keaton, still annoyed about their banishment from the New York stages, had booked a tour of England.
You can't keep the Keatons down!
They were cutting the vacation short and leaving immediately.

Summer went on. Everyone said that Bluffton wasn't the same without the Keatons.
Cobwebs & Rafters seemed sparser and far less lively.

Playing with your friends today?
Nope.
That was the second summer.

The letters from Lex stopped arriving.
HACKLEY PUBLIC LIBRARY
Sometimes I would go to the library and read the vaudeville newspapers.
I learned that the Keatons' tour of England had been cut short. Apparently, Joe didn't like the food.

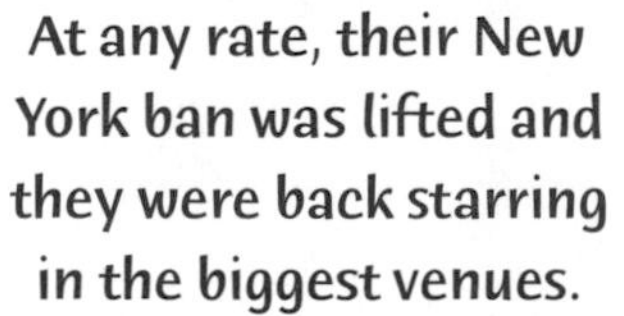
At any rate, their New York ban was lifted and they were back starring in the biggest venues.

BUSTER IS SIXTEEN!

NEW YORK—Vaudeville sensation "Buster" Keaton has reached the grand old age of sixteen. A performer since he was knee-high to a ventriloquist, "Buster" has performed in the finest venues of the vaudeville circuit. As the star of The Three Keatons, "Buster" has been often respectfully referred to as The Human Mop.

That winter, I had other things on my mind.
TALENT SHOW
SHOW US YOUR HIDDEN TALENT!
JANUARY 15
7 P.M.

I had to develop My Act.

JANUARY
1910

CLAP!
clap!
Clap!
CLAP!
CLAP!
TAP
TAP
TAP
TAP
CLAP!
CLAP!
CLAP!
CLAP!
CLAP!
clap!
CLAP!
CLAP
CLAP!
CLAP!
CLAP!
Clap!
CLAP!
CLAP!
CLAP!

CLAP
Clap-clap!
CLAP!
Applause!
CLAP!
Applause!

Pom!

THUD!

Need a hand with the sack, Burt?
Thanks, no. I'll manage fine, Jim. Good day!
Good day to you, Burt. Stay warm, now.
Hi, Henry. What are you up to?
Nothing. Just thought I'd come down here.

I just made some tea. Want to share a sandwich, son?
Thanks.
Slow day so far. Still, it'll probably pick up soon.
Snow's always good for the family business. Shovels and –

What is it, Henry?
I just . . . the family business.
I don't . . . I don't think I want to run the hardware store. When I'm older. I don't want to be a hardware-store owner.

I never expected you to
take over the store, Henry.

Unless that's what you wanted. It's a good business. I took over from your grandfather, that's true.
But I wanted to run the store. It was my choice.
You have a choice, too. You'll have lots of choices to make, Henry.

Don't worry so much about what you are going to do, Henry.
Concentrate on who you are going to be.

Sally!
Um . . .

Well . . .
Henry?
Yes?
It's cold out here.

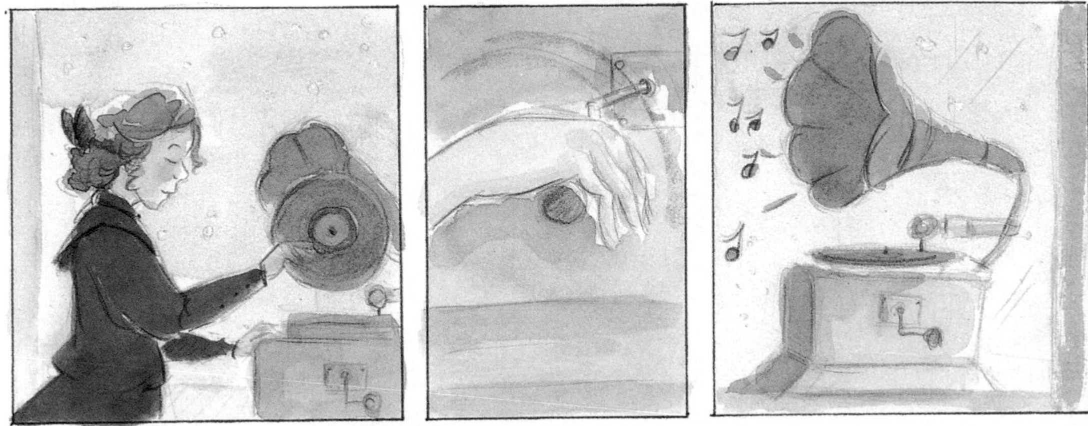

How's your arm?
Better. It's fine. Thanks.

I didn't get a chance to tell you that you were good. At the talent show.
Thank you. I've been playing for seven years now.
Really? I didn't know that.

I take lessons from Mrs. Fisher on Edgewater. She's wonderful. Her husband paints.
He's a painter? I thought he worked in the factory.
He does. But he paints, too. Beautiful pictures. He says he loves to look out at Muskegon Lake and paint the view while his wife plays Chopin.
Isn't that nice?

There's lots of talented folks around here. It's one of the things I love about Muskegon.

You know what else I love?
The library.

JUNE
1910

Did you bring your mitt?

Well, come on.
Summer won't last forever.

ZOOM

HAPPY BIRTHDAY, JOE!!

That was summer in Bluffton.

1927
I chose to stay in
Muskegon when
I got older.
Sally became the
town librarian.
And my wonderful wife.

I bought a small theater near Bluffton and turned it into a movie house.

Now I provide entertainment for everyone in town.

BLUFFTON'S OWN
BUSTER KEATON
STARRING IN
THE GENERAL
And the best comedies of all are made by Buster Keaton.

AUTHOR'S NOTE

Although Henry, Sally, and their families are fictional characters, Buster Keaton and the rest of the vaudevillians were real people. The Actors' Colony at Bluffton, which Joe Keaton founded, existed in Muskegon, Michigan, from 1908–1938. For many years the Keatons were central figures in Bluffton. Buster decided to end the family act in his late teens. He was about to embark on a solo career in vaudeville when he was invited by his friend Roscoe Arbuckle to give the (still relatively new) movies a try. Buster never looked back. He moved to Hollywood and brought his family with him. While this was the beginning of a great era for him professionally, it brought an end to the Keatons' summers in Muskegon.

Buster never forgot Bluffton or his old friends. Lex Neal joined Buster in Hollywood and worked as a writer on some of his movies. Big Joe Roberts and Joe Keaton acted in many of his short films. Buster's movies feature elaborate contraptions and gags, some of which can be traced back to the pranks he concocted during his boyhood summers. While making his movies, Buster would often stop the cameras so that everyone could play a quick game of baseball.

All of Buster's movies are readily available for viewing, and I highly recommend them. They are hilarious, breathtaking, innovative, and will change the way you think about silent films. Buster was a true genius, and his work stands the test of time. In 2007, the American Film Institute included Keaton's *The General* in its list of the 100 greatest American films ever made (it ranked at number 18).

I have been a fan of Buster Keaton since I was a small boy. My brother and I would watch *Cops* and *The General* projected on a bedroom wall by my dad's Super 8 film projector. At first, I just thought he was funny. Then I marveled at the amazing stunts he executed. And then, eventually, I realized he was simply one of the greatest actors and filmmakers who had ever lived. I read everything I could about Buster, including his autobiography, *My Wonderful World of Slapstick*. That is where I discovered the inspiration for this book.

For all his many accomplishments, Buster would always say that the happiest days of his life were those summers he spent at Bluffton.

A teenage Buster in front of Cobwebs & Rafters. Second from the left is Joe Keaton. Big Joe Roberts is behind Buster and Ed Gray is on the far right.

(Date and photographer unknown. From the collection of the author.)